THE REAL
GHOSTBUSTERS™

The Cabinet
of Calimari

Adapted by Maureen Spurgeon
from the original TV script
by Mark Edens and Michael Edens

CARNIVAL

It promised to be a great night out for The Real Ghostbusters. The bright lights of Broadway . . . shiny, big limousines, everyone looking a million dollars . .

It was the Grand Opening Night of the new Magic Theatre, starring The Great Calimari. The Ghostbusters had been invited to attend by the owner himself — Mr Magic. He had sent them free tickets for the best seats in the house.

'Nice of Mr Magic to invite us,' murmured Winston Zeddmore as the curtains drew back and the owner came on stage.

'Yeah . . ' agreed Ray Stantz. 'Too nice. I wonder why he did?'

'Ladies and Gentlemen,' Mr Magic announced, 'The Magic Theatre is proud to present that master of illusion – The Great Calimari!'

Behind him stood a tall figure dressed impressively in a huge, sweeping cloak and top hat. He was accompanied by a blonde girl, who sparkled with sequins and who he introduced as 'My assistant Vanna'.

The Ghostbusters were determined not to miss a trick. Their eyes were glued on Calimari – there was no way he was going to fool *them*. The magician was holding his hand in front of a large mirror. He rapped on it three times and then turned towards Vanna, waving his hands in front of her

face. Her eyes fluttered and then closed. Then, in one dramatic movement, The Great Calimari swept his hands high above his head and then brought them down, pointing theatrically at her feet. There was a puff of smoke and Vanna disappeared into thin air.

Calimari rapped three more times on the mirror and Vanna's reflection appeared, out of nowhere. He held his hand out towards her and she stepped out of the mirror, larger than life and with her arms raised to acknowledge the thunderous applause from the audience.

'Know something?' whispered Ray to Egon. 'I swear I know that trick.'

'It's all done with mirrors,' Egon replied.

But even he had to admit that The Great Calimari knew how to put on a performance. Vanna was now blindfolding Calimari and fastening him into a straightjacket and handcuffs. A hush descended throughout the entire theatre as a chain around his feet hoisted him upside down, above a huge glass tank. Vanna, accompanied by a long drum-roll, pulled a lever and began to lower him head first towards the water.

Suddenly there were gasps of horror from the audience which quickly turned into terrified screams. When Calimari heard them, he shook off his blindfold and found himself looking down into a seething mass of boiling water in the tank below.

'Help!' he shouted in blind panic. 'Vanna!'

Vanna carried on smiling sweetly at the audience, oblivious to The Great Calimari, who was trying desperately to struggle out of his straightjacket.

'Pull the lever,' he yelled to her. 'Pull the lever!'

She finally got the message and yanked the lever, bringing The Great Calimari to a halt only inches from the boiling water. The Ghostbusters were amazed to see that the water was filled with a horrible wailing fiend who throbbed and pulsed, getting brighter and brighter . . .

The water bubbled and boiled more and more violently and then, with an almighty CRASH, the tank exploded, sending thousands of gallons of water gushing out into the audience like a tidal wave.

Sitting in the front row, The Ghostbusters were in direct line of fire. Although soaked, Peter Venkmann wasn't complaining. With a frightened 'Ooooh!' the lovely Vanna had been swept right onto his lap. The others watched the stage as, with a flash of light and a deafening clap of thunder, the green glow in the tank disappeared. Now they knew why Mr Magic had invited them. He had some gruesome ghostly gremlins, that was for sure.

The Great Calimari was left swinging back and forth on his chain, like a dripping wet pendulum, until a stagehand went to his rescue. By the time

The Ghostbusters had got backstage, there was a terrific argument going on.

'You're washed up, Calimari!' thundered Mr Magic.

Peter shook water from his hair and squished his feet around in his sodden shoes. 'Join the club!' he growled. 'And I thought we were just going to have fun this time!'

'Now you know why I invited you here tonight,' Mr Magic told them. 'When the ghost started to appear at rehearsals, Calimari said he could handle it.'

'I *can* handle it!' Calimari insisted. 'I don't

'need any help.'

'I'm giving you one last chance Calimari!' stormed Mr Magic. 'If The Ghostbusters can get rid of the ghost, I'll keep you on! Otherwise, you're through!'

Calimari sighed. 'I guess,' he said, 'you give me no choice.'

It didn't take long for The Ghostbusters to think up a plan. Proton Packs and Guns at the ready, Egon and Winston decided to check backstage.

'Do you think there's anything to this magic stuff?' wondered Winston, with a dubious glance at Calimari's mirror.

'Of course not,' snapped Egon, his intelligence insulted.

Egon and Winston began their inspection in earnest. They were so absorbed in what they were doing that they didn't notice Calimari's reflection, which had appeared in the mirror. Nor did they notice Calimari stepping out from the mirror – his hands gesturing at them as though he was performing a magic trick.

'I didn't believe in ghosts before I took this job!' Winston chattered on. He glanced about him and noticed that a box that Calimari used to saw Vanna in half still had a sword sticking out of it. Suddenly the sword sprung into the air, reverberating with a ghostly BOING!

'Look out!' yelled Winston, diving for cover inside a nearby apple-shaped cabinet. Egon wasn't so lucky. The saw flew towards him, slicing clean through the cable from his Proton Gun to Proton Pack, sending sparks shooting out in all directions. At the same moment, Winston's cabinet slammed shut, revealing the words 'Death of a Hundred Swords' written on the door.

Egon stepped back in astonishment as Calimari appeared before him, his arms raised in command.

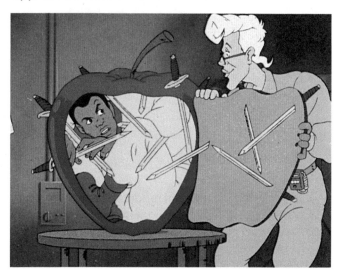

A dozen more swords obeyed his order and leapt out of a nearby basket to fly through the air and plunge into the cabinet.

With both his Proton Gun and Proton Pack out of action, Egon was powerless to defend himself. All he could do was turn and run as fast as he could from the remaining flying saw. He dived into a stage curtain in an attempt to hide. But it was no good — the saw continued after him, slicing and

jabbing at the curtain until it had cut out an image
of Egon. By some miracle, Egon escaped. But, only
just. The next minute the saw had driven through
the heart of his cloth image, pinning it firmly to the
wall.

A strange silence descended on the theatre as
Calimari walked back into the mirror and
disappeared. Then a sinister whisper echoed
around the walls, 'You haven't heard the last of The
Great Calimari!'

'We'd better warn Ray and Peter,' Egon decided
with one last, worried look at the saw. 'This
situation is beginning to look distinctly dangerous.'

'That sure is some understatement,' came a

muffled cry from the cabinet. Egon had forgotten
that Winston was still shut inside. When he opened
it up, there he was, all twisted up from dodging the
blades of the razor-sharp swords. Talk about a
close shave!
Backstage Peter was hoping that Vanna could help
with some information.

  'We'd like to talk to you about tonight's
performance . . .' he began, but all she did was
smile vacantly at him.

  'What makes you think I know anything?' she
said in a monotone, and shut the door in his face.

  'Good question!' said Ray to the door, before he
and Peter went to join the others. As soon as they

were out of the way, Calimari appeared and knocked on the door.

'Look into my eyes!' he commanded when Vanna answered, and then he fixed her to the spot with his mad, evil stare. Within a matter of seconds, her eyes had become like saucers, wide and unblinking. She had been hypnotised. Calimari nodded, satisfied. Now she wouldn't be able to tell anybody anything . . .

Meanwhile Ray's PKE meter was bleeping frantically. Something spooky was very near. Sure enough, there was a flash of light, an earth-shattering clap of thunder, and then . . . the thing from the tank appeared from nowhere. It beckoned mysteriously to The Ghostbusters.

'I think it wants to talk,' said Ray, edging forward, pluckily. 'Er – hello. I'm Ray Stantz.'

'Look out Ray!' Winston interrupted. He had raised his Proton Gun and fired at the ghost before Ray had chance to turn around. He was right on target. Egon rushed forward with the Ghost Trap and immediately the ghost was sucked inside, the last of its wails gradually fading. An easy job well done. Or was it?

'I was about to communicate with him,' complained Ray, but the others barely heard. They were all staring at the Ghost Trap, silently watching it grow brighter and brighter. None of them had ever seen anything like it. The doors of the Ghost Trap burst open, and a dazzling column of light shot out, carrying the ghost with it. It hurtled towards the ceiling.

'How did he do that?' Ray asked, staring in

astonishment at the ceiling. SPLAT! A large dollop of slime plopped onto his upturned face.

'Must be a defective trap,' suggested Egon, after some thought. 'Let's try another one.'

But the same thing happened again; the ghost shot out of the new trap like a jack-in-the-box.

'I'll get *another* trap,' said Winston wearily.

As before, they trapped the ghost easily enough, but this time Peter was taking no chances. He secured the trap with chains and a padlock. But it was no good, the chains rattled off and a column of bright light shot out. The ghost had escaped again!

'Th-this guy should have his own act!' Peter panted, as all The Ghostbusters chased it along the corridor. 'He's a better escape artist than Calimari!'

'There he is!' yelled Egon.

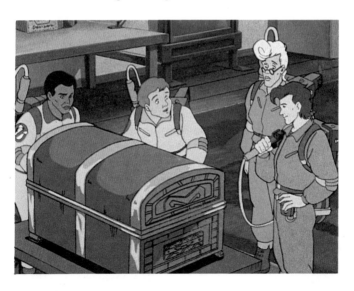

'He's going into Calimari's dressing room!' shouted Winston.

The only sound as The Ghostbusters entered the dressing room was the bleeping of Ray's PKE meter.

'I'm getting a PKE reading from this trunk!' he yelled, tugging at its lid. 'I think there must be something inside it. Can anyone pick a lock?'

Peter didn't want to waste time messing around with locks. Instead, he raised his Proton Gun and blasted the lid right off the trunk. The Ghostbusters peered inside. But there was nothing but a collection of old, faded theatre posters, and just one press-cutting, tucked away in the corner. Peter left the room with a snort of disgust, impatient with Egon for bothering to pick the press cutting up.

The cutting had a photo of Calimari beside a headline, *MAGICIAN JAILED IN UNEXPLAINED DISAPPEARANCE.* Egon read out the rest of the article, his specs beginning to sparkle. *'The Great Calimari asked for a volunteer from the audience to disappear in his Cabinet of Mystery . . . and . . . the volunteer was never seen again!'*

'I knew there was something fishy about him,' said Winston.

By now Peter had reached Vanna's dressing room door. He was hoping for a slightly more friendly reception than last time. And, although her eyes looked strangely distant, she seemed quite pleased to see him.

'I've been expecting you,' she told Peter cooly.

'But, I think we should go somewhere more private.' She waved a slender hand towards a brightly-coloured, carved wooden booth, which was standing with its door wide open. On the front, out of sight, were painted the words, 'Cabinet of Mystery'.

'Whatever you say,' grinned Peter, stepping inside. 'There's not much room, but I think I can squeeze you in here.'

But as soon as Vanna saw that Peter was safely in the cabinet, she slammed the door shut. Almost immediately the whole theatre was shaken to its foundations by a violent clap of thunder.

Egon, Winston and Ray heard the noise and came tearing through the theatre to see what had happened. They burst into Vanna's dressing room and rushed inside.

'Where's Peter?' asked Ray.

Without speaking, Vanna pointed to the Cabinet of Mystery. Right on cue, the door creaked open, revealing — nothing at all. Nothing but emptiness. He had completely disappeared. The other Ghostbusters looked at each other with expressions of horror — this was the same Cabinet of Mystery that featured in the press cutting.

'Peter should've known better than to go in there!' cried Ray. 'What could possibly have made him do such a stupid thing?'

They glanced at each other, and then, one by one, they turned to look at Vanna. She stared back at them without saying a word.

'Notice the vacant stare?' said Egon after a pause, waving his hand in front of her face. 'She's been hypnotised! And there's only one person who could have done it. The Great Calimari!'

There was not a moment to lose. Egon, Winston and Ray raced straight back to Calimari's dressing room to wait for him. They didn't have to wait long. Calimari burst into the room and before he even realised they were there, he began to examine the wreck of his precious trunk.

'We have to talk to you Calimari,' began Egon.

'You have to tell us how to get Peter out of the Cabinet of Mystery,' thundered Ray.

Calimari folded his arms across his chest and turned his back to The Ghostbusters so that they could not see his face. He knew they would know he was lying if they caught his expression.

'I — I can't. As long as the ghost is on the loose, your friend is trapped!'

'Then,' said Egon, 'we'll catch it — if that's what is needed to get Peter out of that thing. But, if you are lying . . .'

'We'll be back,' finished Ray, grimly.

Calimari waited until the door had closed, then he pulled out a suitcase from behind his dressing table.

'They'll never catch *him*,' he predicted, his lips set in a thin line.

But, what had happened to Peter? The moment Vanna had slammed the cabinet door tight shut, he had found himself plunged into darkness, walking and walking, on and on, until he came to a vast room full of enormous pieces of furniture.

'Is there anybody here?' he called out. An echo

answered him mournfully.

'Is there anybody here? Here . . .? Here . . .?'

'This is Peter Venkman.'

'Peter, who? Who . . .? Who . . .?'

He stopped, turning his head one way, and then another. 'There's something strange about this place,' he muttered.

Meanwhile, PKE readings on the PKE meter had led the other three Ghostbusters to the loading bay at

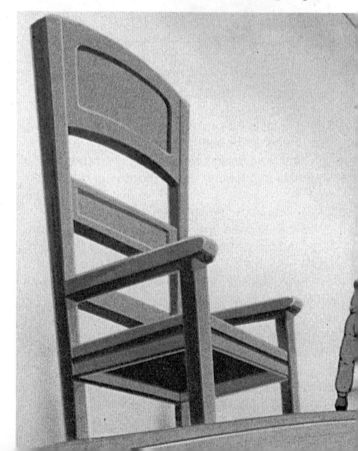

the back of the theatre. Ray hid behind a pile of scenery and waited until Egon, who had taken up his position behind a pile of crates, gave him the 'thumbs up' signal. The ghost was about to make another dramatic appearance!

It hardly got the chance to start floating around, before Ray jumped to his feet and fired his Proton Gun. Egon shot simultaneously and the ghost was caught in the cross-fire of ion streams.

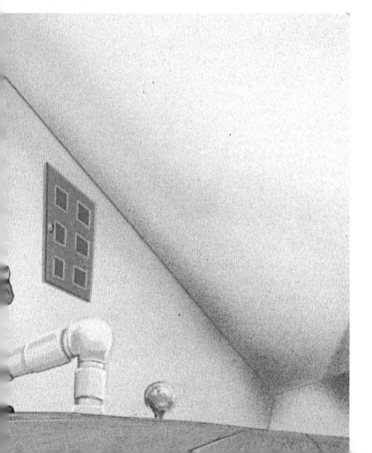

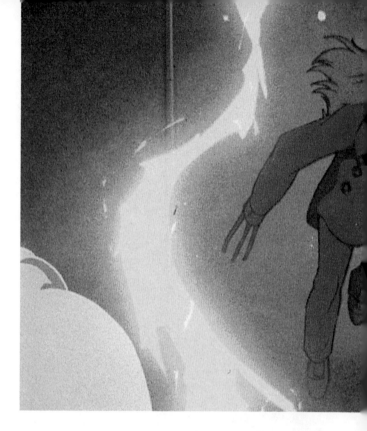

'Get him over that box, Ray!' shouted Egon, indicating a large wooden construction with wires shooting out in all directions. 'I've set the Ghost Trap, right inside.'

There were no more hitches. Egon stepped on the remote control pedal, the Ghost Trap opened . . . and with one last, desperate wail, the ghost was sucked inside.

'Okay, Winston,' bellowed Ray. There was a loud rumble as Winston arrived, backing a cement mixer

through the door to the loading bay. Egon and Ray
knew that Winston was a good driver. Even so,
they held their breath until he had positioned the
cement chute directly over the box, filling it right up
to the top with a load of wet concrete. Winston
switched off the engine with a flourish. Ray and
Egon looked very pleased with themselves.

'That should hold him!' pronounced Egon as he
watched Ray smoothing over the concrete with a
trowel.

The trouble was they still had no idea where to start looking for Peter. Little did they know that, at that very moment, he was walking across an area of dry, bare land, with only a few limp, twisted trees for company.

'I feel like I'm being watched,' he muttered to himself. And sure enough, there in the background, and unseen by him, was a single eye.

'Wonder how long I've been in here?' An hour-glass began floating around behind him. He didn't see that either. But he did happen to spot a small stone lying on the ground in front of him. And, as he bent down to pick it up, a window began floating high above his head. Without thinking, he tossed the stone aside. The sound of breaking glass made him turn round in surprise . . . in front of him was a smashed pane of glass. Wherever he was, it was most peculiar and very, very strange.

Suddenly he tripped up and toppled over. He fell to the floor but then went on falling, down and down and down . . . When he finally landed, it was on something very soft and spongy. He looked down and saw that it was a clock-face, draped over a piece of rock like a Surrealist painting.

'You must be Peter what's-his-name,' a voice called over to him. 'I heard the echo talking about you.'

Peter was being addressed by a small, podgy little man with a bald head and wearing a business suit.

'My name's Irving,' smiled the stranger. 'I was at a magic show, and they asked for a volunteer from the audience, so I raised my hand . . .'

'How long have you been here?' Peter interrupted.

'Beats me,' said Irving. 'There's something wrong with my watch.'

Before Peter could ask him another question, they both felt the ground beneath their feet start to shake and slide. Peter grabbed hold of the nearest tree and clung on tightly. Irving was not so lucky.

'Nice meeting you, Peter!' he called out, his voice fading as he plummeted into the distance.

Meanwhile, The Great Calimari was getting the Cabinet of Mystery on its side, so that he could load it onto a trolley. That was why they were all tumbling about inside. Then, he threw his trunk and his suitcase on top of the cabinet, and got behind the trolley, ready to push.

'Open the door, Vanna,' he commanded. She obeyed without a word. But his path was blocked by Ray who was waiting outside in the corridor.

'Hold it, Calimari! Where do you think you're going?'

'We've caught the ghost,' announced Egon, slapping the top of the concrete, now set rock hard into a solid block.

'So tell us how to get Peter out of The Cabinet of Mystery!' shouted Winston.

'If I knew that,' answered Calimari with an air of exasperating calm, 'it wouldn't be a mystery.'

Silence fell. The three Ghostbusters bunched together, standing side by side, making it impossible for Calimari to get past. Then Ray spoke. His voice was dangerously cold.

'You aren't going anywhere,' he told Calimari,

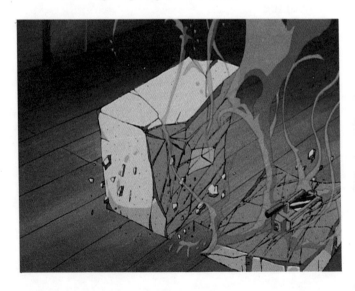

'until we get Peter back!'

By this time, Calimari was a desperate man. 'You can't stop me!' he croaked, pushing the heavy cabinet straight at The Ghostbusters as he spoke. Somehow they all managed to dodge it. They watched in astonishment as, with an ear-splitting crash, the Cabinet of Mystery smashed into the block of cement, cracking it clean in two.

From its depths, a bright glaring light began to appear. It became wider and bigger, blazing out of the crack. And with it came the ghost.

'No!' Calimari screamed as the ghost headed straight for him. It was a very frightened man who ran like the wind down the corridor, pale and trembling, with the ghost at his heels.

'Stop that ghost!' yelled Ray, his Proton Gun already blazing. But rather than hit their target, the Ion Streams slammed into the trunk at full blast, exploding the cabinet and the suitcase, as well. The Ghostbusters ducked as a mass of posters and newspapers, and Calimari's stage clothes flew around the corridor, swirling wildly before floating down to the floor.

When everything was calm the three Ghostbusters suddenly realised that Vanna had come out of her dressing room. They all gathered together and looked at the trunk, which had almost been wrecked by the explosion. Suddenly Egon noticed a secret door at the bottom of the trunk. 'Hey,' he cried. 'Look at this!'

The door was already half open. As Egon stooped to pick the trunk up, a notebook slipped from the hidden compartment and fell to the floor.

'So there *was* a false bottom!' Egon murmured, as he picked up the notebook. 'Secret notes,' he read, peering at the writing on the cover. 'Keep Out! Harry Houdini.'

The others were too stunned to utter a word.

'Houdini! Of course,' Egon continued, 'the world famous escape artist! Nobody could trap *him*!'

Ray gave a low whistle. '*That's* why Calimari's tricks seemed so familiar! They were the same tricks Houdini used to do!'

'Yeah,' nodded Winston. 'Stolen from Houdini's secret notebook!'

'Then that must be the ghost of Harry Houdini!' said Egon. 'Hasn't lost his touch, has he?'

Before anyone else could say anything, there was a rush of air behind them. The Ghostbusters spun round and saw the ghost hovering in the air.

'Look out guys!' shouted Winston, taking aim with his Proton Gun.

'Wait a minute,' said Ray, a restraining hand on Winston's arm. 'I think he wants the notebook.' The ghost held out his hand imploringly as Ray walked towards him. 'If Calimari stole Houdini's notebook,' he was saying, 'he may also have stolen the Cabinet of Mystery . . . And if its Houdini's cabinet, the ghost might be able to get Peter out . . .'

Egon and Winston held their breath as Ray handed over the notebook to the ghost of Harry Houdini, who was nodding as though he knew what he had to do. As soon as the notebook was in his hands, there was a deafening thunder clap as the ghost flew towards the cabinet. The

Ghostbusters watched in amazement as it disappeared through the solid wall.

'No wonder Calimari didn't want to co-operate with us,' mused Egon. 'He was afraid Houdini's ghost would tell us about the notebook he stole.'

'It must have been Calimari who made that saw attack us . . .' Winston's words were cut short by a loud crack as the Cabinet door burst open. The Ghostbusters were speechless as a podgy little man with a bald head appeared. He glanced around him and said, 'I'd better call my wife. She's probably waiting up for me. Anyone got a dime?'

'It's a quarter now!' said Winston.

'A quarter!' The little man shook his head as he spoke. 'Maybe I should have stayed in the cabinet.'

The three dumbfoundeed Ghostbusters watched the man as he walked along the corridor.

'Is Irving there?' Peter's voice shattered the silence.

'Peter!' cried the others, as he poked his head out of the cabinet.

'Look out!' Vanna suddenly shouted. The Ghostbusters spun round and saw Calimari running towards them. He threw himself at them, obviously trying to push them into the Cabinet of Mystery. But, just in time, they managed to dodge out of the way. Calimari tried to stop but couldn't. He continued to charge forwards, tripping over the open door as he did so and finally falling slap bang into the Cabinet of Mystery.

The door slammed shut behind him, accompanied by an enormous clap of thunder. The Great Calimari had gone for good.

'Maybe Houdini will let him out some time,' Winston said thoughtfully.

Back at Ghostbusters' HQ, Peter put his mind to the remaining problem. How to bring Vanna out of her trance. He had tried everything he could think of, but nothing had worked.

'Come on, Peter,' said Winston, at last. 'How are you going to break the hypnosis with Calimari gone?'

Peter smiled. 'You ever seen ''Sleeping Beauty''?' he asked leaning across to kiss Vanna's cheek. There was only a moment's pause before Vanna opened her eyes, blinking just a little, and then smiling so sweetly that Peter's heart skipped a beat.

'Thank you,' she sighed. 'Gee, Calimari said the only way anyone else could bring me out of that, was if I kissed a toad! So where did you find a toad in New York?'

Carnival
An imprint of the Children's Division
of the Collins Publishing Group
8 Grafton Street, London W1X 3LA

Published by Carnival 1989

Reprinted 1989 twice

Copyright © 1989 by Columbia Pictures Television,
a division of CPT Holdings, Inc.
THE REAL GHOSTBUSTERS™ Television series Copyright
©1984 by Columbia Pictures Industries, Inc.

GHOSTBUSTERS logo and logo design are
licensed trademarks from Columbia Pictures Industries, Inc.

ISBN 0 00 194917 9

Printed and bound in Great Britain by
PURNELL BOOK PRODUCTION LIMITED
A member of BPCC plc